River of Amber

by Linda Baxter

COVER-TO-COVER BOOKS

Perfection Learning®

Cover illustration: Sue F. Cornelison
Inside illustration: Larassa Kabel

For Raisa

About the Author

Linda Baxter was born in Cheyenne, Wyoming, and traveled with her military family, finally settling in Tempe, Arizona. She graduated with a degree in elementary education from Arizona State University. Ms. Baxter taught elementary grades in Phoenix, Arizona, and Catshill, Bromsgrove, England.

She lives with her husband, Dave, and three children in Monte Sereno, California.

Text © 2001 by Perfection Learning® Corporation.
All rights reserved. No part of this book may be used or reproduced in any manner whatsoever without written permission from the publisher.
Printed in the United States of America.
For information, contact

Perfection Learning® Corporation
1000 North Second Avenue, P.O. Box 500
Logan, Iowa 51546-0500
Phone: 1-800-831-4190
Fax: 1-712-644-2392

Paperback ISBN 0-7891-5394-7
Cover Craft® ISBN 0-7807-9804-x

Printed in the U.S.A.

Contents

Introduction

The year 1939 was a momentous one in European history. **Adolf Hitler** had assembled a terrifying war machine in Germany. He had already overrun Austria and Czechoslovakia. He now threatened Poland with invasion. England and France were afraid to challenge him, fearing the destruction of another world war. No one knew that Hitler and **Joseph Stalin**, the dictator of Russia, were now planning to invade the Baltic States (Latvia, Estonia, and Lithuania). Little Latvia would lose her freedom in the grip of Russia and Germany.

Europe in 1939

1

Racing the Wind

"I have the main sheet!" shouted Sasha above the wind.

"Pull it hard. That's good," called Laddy over his shoulder. "Now lash it to the cleat."

Sasha pulled the thick rope with all his strength. He ducked as the boom swung to the starboard side of the 35-foot sloop. With a quick yank, he looped the rope over the metal cleat. A brisk spring wind cut into his cheeks.

They turned the sailboat into the morning sun. For a moment, the amber light reflecting off the bay blinded them. Sasha shaded his eyes with one hand. He braced himself against the pitch of the sailboat. The craft rode the wave, its bow high. Then it dropped again through the swell. Laddy glanced at Sasha and grinned.

"You're getting to be a better sailor every time we come out. Soon I'll let you take her by yourself," said Laddy.

Sasha settled next to him in the stern. Laddy carefully adjusted the angle of the sail. He guided the sailboat to the far shore, running ahead of the wind.

"I'm ready," agreed Sasha. He took the tiller from Laddy.

The river's current grew stronger as they approached the open water of the gulf. Their destination was near. Sasha could pick out the small beach surrounded by tall pines. The beach was deserted as usual.

"Turn her out of the wind?" asked Sasha.

"Yes, in a moment. Ready? Now!" shouted Laddy. "Great!" The sail fluttered in the breeze. The boat crept closer to shore.

Laddy jumped over the side. The boat began to scrape the sandy bottom of the shore. He grabbed the bowline and drew the boat from the gentle swell. Sasha lowered the sail.

He joined Laddy in the water. The current tugged at Sasha's legs. Although it had been a warm March, the water was still icy cold. Sasha and Laddy moved quickly.

Together they beached the craft. They tied her bow to a tree trunk with sturdy ropes. Then they sat down in the sand to catch their breath.

"It's more fun when you come, Sasha," puffed Laddy. He lay back on the warm sand. "I can never get her out of the current here on my own. You are a good first mate."

Laddy pushed his short dark curls off his thin face. He had deep brown eyes—almost black. He warmed his tall frame in the shimmering sand.

Laddy had recently returned home after finishing his university studies. Sasha was younger, but Laddy never reminded him of the five years that separated them.

"I'm starving. What did Raisa pack us for lunch?" asked Laddy.

Sasha stood and headed back to the boat. He lifted the lunch basket from the small hold.

"I saw her put in some fresh bread," Sasha said. He

peeked into the basket. "Hey, look!" he called out. "There's cold salmon, a tin of caviar, and a jar of peaches. We're in luck." Sasha set the wicker basket between them on the sand.

"Good," agreed Laddy, digging through the basket. "There's a cider for you and one for me."

Laddy unwrapped the bottles from their dish towels. "You have a good big sister, Sasha. I'm lucky my big brother married her.

"Happy Naming Day, Sasha," Laddy toasted. Today was the feast of St. Alexander, Sasha's patron saint. Sasha's given name was **Alexander Victorovich Bausch**. Tonight his family would celebrate with cake and presents. It was a Latvian tradition.

"Thanks," replied Sasha.

Sasha broke the bread into crusty chunks. Vladimir, whom everyone called Laddy, opened the small tin of caviar. The cider stung the back of Sasha's throat as he swallowed.

"People in other countries pay a lot of money for caviar. Did you know that?" asked Laddy with a big bite in his mouth.

"Really?" questioned Sasha. Sasha loved the salty fish eggs. They were a popular food in Russia. He didn't understand why they would be expensive in other places.

"Yes. I read it in the American paper. I'm trying to improve my English," said Laddy.

Sasha made a face. "I have to start with an English tutor soon. Raisa is insisting. I told her four languages were enough."

"Four?" questioned Laddy.

"Russian and French at home, German at school, and Latvian, of course," Sasha pointed out.

"Yes, but the English will come in handy," insisted Laddy.

"At least I'll be able to understand the American movies," Sasha agreed. They sat in the sun, enjoying the cool breeze on a warm spring day.

"How is it living with your sister and George?" asked Laddy, changing the subject. "Do they baby you too much?"

"George is fine. He and I get along. He's not home much, anyway. He works so hard at the factory. Raisa is busy with my little nephew. I try to stay out of the way," answered Sasha. He shrugged his shoulders.

"You're not in the way," argued Laddy. "It was your sister's idea, you know. I told her there were good boarding schools. She would have none of it. She wanted you to come live in our home."

This made Sasha feel better. He didn't want to be away from his family—what was left of it. Two years ago, Sasha's father had died. Sasha had been 15. His mother had never been allowed to leave Moscow. She seemed so far away. His sister was his only family now.

Sasha squashed the nagging feeling of worry. His mother had not written in several months. Sasha knew that something was wrong. Sometimes the fear almost overwhelmed him. Where was she? What was happening?

But there was little he could do. He pushed the worries to the back of his mind. Today was for sailing.

Laddy took a final swig of his cider. He stuck the glass bottle upside down in the sand. The sailboat bumped against the shore in a rhythmic beat. Sasha felt sleepy from the food and the sun.

"Come on, lazybones. Let's go for a run," prodded Laddy. He jumped to his feet. "We can't lie around here all day."

"Will the boat be all right?" asked Sasha. He stretched and brushed the sand off his legs.

"There is no one for miles on this stretch of the river. If we run along the shore, we can keep her in sight," Laddy assured him.

"Sounds good," agreed Sasha as he jumped up. He began to sprint down the beach. He had a three-step lead on Laddy in no time. Soon Sasha had left him behind.

"Wait," called Laddy, laughing and puffing. "You don't have to win the Olympics today. I just wanted a nice, friendly run."

"You know I can't run any way but fast," Sasha

called back. He made several wide circles in the sand to wait for Laddy. Finally, Laddy caught up.

They jogged along the river's edge. Sasha stopped at the end of the beach. A large boulder interrupted the flow of sand.

Laddy climbed onto the rock for a better view. "Now, Sasha. You sprint back as fast as you can. I'll time you. Ready?" asked Laddy.

Sasha positioned himself for a fast start. He gave a quick nod. Laddy looked at his watch and shouted, "Go!"

Sasha raced down the beach. Little puffs of sand flew into the air. His feet dug in for speed. Sasha felt his body surge forward. His heart raced and his lungs screamed. He quickly returned to the sailboat landing.

"Sasha!" shouted Laddy from his perch. "You took a full five seconds off your last time. Great job!"

Sasha waved and then bent over with his hands on his knees. He took a moment to catch his breath.

Laddy trotted back to Sasha. He clapped him soundly on the back. "If you keep that up, you'll make the national team," said Laddy proudly.

"That's the idea," said Sasha. "But I still have to get my time under 54 seconds to qualify. Williams won the 400-meter in the 1936 games with a time of 46.5 seconds."

Laddy whistled softly.

"I know," agreed Sasha. "It's a tough time to beat. But I still want to try."

"There's a better chance I can go now that the games have been changed from Tokyo to Helsinki," said Sasha. "I already have part of the fare saved. From work last summer."

"Tokyo was a long way," said Laddy.

"They changed the location because of the war between Japan and China," explained Sasha.

"I just hope things stay calm in Europe," worried Laddy out loud.

In the late afternoon, Sasha wandered down to the water. He searched for the small yellow stones that littered the shore. He bent to pick up a few of the clear golden pebbles. Sasha studied each individually before tossing most into the black water.

"You always look for those stones," said Laddy. He rested in the shade of a small birch tree. "What do you do with all that amber? None of it is worth much."

"I like the ones with little bugs in them. Those creatures lived millions of years ago," Sasha said. He held up a pebble-sized chunk of amber. A small insect was trapped inside.

"Imagine being preserved for all those years in a bit of sap," he said. "Then a strange being from another time picks you up and puts you in his pocket."

Laddy shook his head.

"I know. Raisa thinks I'm crazy too," chuckled Sasha. He collected the golden fossils. "She had to get me another box to keep my amber. I filled up the first one. But I only keep the ones with bugs. Who knows—maybe I'll discover a new insect someday. Look, this one has two little bugs in there. See?"

"Come on, Sasha. Time to head back," said Laddy as he stood. "That sister of yours and brother of mine are expecting us for dinner. If we're late again, George will shout the roof off."

Sasha held out his hand to check the wind. The late afternoon sun sparkled across the small waves. It lit only the very tops of the crests.

"You're right. The wind is calming. We'd better hurry, or we'll be stuck out in the middle of the river. I don't want George to have to come looking for us again," Sasha said. He waded into the river.

Laddy and Sasha stowed the basket. They pushed the boat back into the current. Sasha untied the lines. He jumped into the boat, grabbing the tiller.

Laddy hoisted the sail. The breeze caught them. Soon they were skimming over the water back to **Riga**.

2

Into the Wind

Raisa looked out the kitchen window. Laddy and Sasha were climbing the back courtyard steps.

"You two better come in and clean up for dinner. Hurry. Our company will be here any minute," Raisa called through the open window.

Sasha could smell dinner cooking. "Sorry we're late," he apologized as he came in the back door. "The wind didn't calm down until late in the afternoon."

Raisa smiled slightly. She was only mildly annoyed. Then she scolded, "It does that every afternoon. I think it's just a good excuse to stay out a bit longer."

Laddy smiled. "You have us there. But your cooking is worth coming home for. Mmm, pork roast with apples." He sniffed the air appreciatively.

"I'll be on time for dinner," he promised. He raced up the back stairs.

Sasha hurried to change into clean clothes. He finished tying his tie and slipped into his good jacket. Then he galloped back down the stairs.

There was loud knocking on the door. Sasha hurried to answer it.

"Hello, Sasha," greeted Ralph and Dieter. "Happy Naming Day to you. Is dinner ready?"

"Mind your manners, Dieter," Sasha teased his friend.

"Yeah, mind your manners. Or we won't get invited again. I like to come here for dinner," said Ralph.

"If you want manners, I'll show you manners," said Dieter.

Raisa entered the hall. She called to the boys, "Come on in. Hello, Ralph, Dieter."

"Good evening to you, Raisa. May I say you look very beautiful tonight," said Dieter in an over-dignified manner. He had very pale blond hair that was cut short. His blue eyes shone brightly. He took Raisa's hand. Then Dieter kissed it as he clicked his heels together smartly.

Ralph and Sasha hooted. Raisa pulled her hand away.

"Where did you learn that?" laughed Sasha.

Dieter grinned. "I saw the **headmaster** do it when he greeted some dignitary's wife."

Raisa grinned and said to the boys, "A few good manners couldn't hurt. Sasha, will you bring in the bread basket? I'll show your friends to the table."

"Sure," said Sasha. He retrieved the basket of rolls from the wooden table in the kitchen.

A big chocolate cake stood on the table. Sasha's name was written in white icing on top. He took a tiny taste of the frosting. Smiling, he returned to his family.

Raisa had placed her small son, Larik, in a tall chair next to her. Her husband, George, sat at the end of the table. Ralph and Dieter sat across from Sasha and Laddy.

Raisa ladled cold **borscht**. She topped each bowl with sour cream.

"Mmm," said Sasha. "You know, Larik. When I was little like you, I used to call this pink soup."

As the soup was passed, George asked, "Sasha, when do you begin track practice again? You've had two weeks off. Right?"

Dieter responded first. "We've had two weeks off, but I caught Sasha out running along the road twice."

"Did you run on your own every day?" asked Ralph. "Or did the coach tell you to?"

"I like to run," answered Sasha with a shrug. "If I stop even for a few days, I lose time. I want that spot on the Latvian National Team. I have to get my time down ten more seconds."

George nodded.

"Sasha run fast," chirped little Larik.

"I hope so," laughed Sasha.

Dieter asked, "Did you hear Hitler's speech on the radio last night? My father was so upset. But I don't see what the problem is. Do you, Sasha? Hitler has all the Germans working again. They were starving after the war. That's what I heard."

"My parents were upset too," chimed in Ralph. "They didn't say anything, but I could tell."

George nodded and said, "Hitler may have the German people working again. But at what cost? He is building a military machine. When he finishes, he will set it on all of us."

Laddy agreed, "I don't trust the man. He makes promises he will not keep and threats that he will."

Ralph argued, "Well, we don't have to worry. What would he want with little Latvia? We don't have much."

"We have a port," George pointed out. "And access to Russia. Riga has always been an important location on the Baltic Sea."

Laddy added, "Well, even Hitler wouldn't think to challenge Stalin. That would be suicide."

"Hitler will challenge us all," Raisa predicted.

A cold silence fell over the diners. Suddenly Sasha wasn't very hungry—even for chocolate cake.

After dinner, Raisa cleaned little Larik's face with a damp cloth. Then she washed each sticky hand. Larik fussed at being scrubbed so thoroughly.

Sasha tried to make Larik feel better. "Do you want to go for an airplane ride?" he asked. "Get your hands all clean. Then I'll take you flying up the stairs to bed."

Larik beamed up at Sasha. He held still so his mother could finish. Then he stood on the chair with arms raised. "Airplane, Sasha," demanded Larik.

Sasha grabbed him around the middle. "Now make your wings," instructed Sasha. Larik positioned his arms. "There you go. You need big wings to get up that mountain. Start your engine." Both boys roared their engines. Sasha flew Larik up the stairs.

"More!" squealed Larik.

"One flight a night," called Raisa. She laughed from halfway up the staircase.

Sasha planted two kisses on his airplane's forehead

and said, "Goodnight, Larik Airplane. One for now and one for later."

Sasha headed down to join Laddy and his friends. George and Raisa stayed upstairs to put Larik to bed.

Ralph leaned back in the easy chair. The open windows let in the night air. City noises from below drifted into the room. They could hear people walking and a streetcar clanging.

The fireplace stood cold. It wasn't needed on the warm evening. Sasha slumped on the couch.

"Have you heard about the new chemistry master?" asked Sasha. "Do you know who has taken the position?"

Ralph shrugged his shoulders. "I haven't heard. But he couldn't be any worse than old Porkoff."

Dieter chipped in, "Imagine a chemistry teacher who can't see past his beakers." The boys laughed.

"I just hope he teaches us something," Sasha said. "I need that exam to complete my acceptance at the university."

"I bet you could teach us more than Porkoff," Dieter said.

"I just hope I pass," Ralph said. "My father was so angry last term."

"Well, you did get the lowest score ever on the final test. Three points! You get three points for getting your name right," said Sasha.

"And that was all I knew on that test," Ralph hooted.

Sasha said, "Just watch me. I'll get you through."

"Do you want to go to a party at Sonia's tonight?" asked Ralph. "Your sister won't care if you go, will she? I think Sonia likes you." Ralph nudged Sasha.

"Thanks, but not tonight," answered Sasha. "I need to be ready for track practice tomorrow. When I went to the last party with you, I didn't get home until daylight."

"Was Raisa angry?" asked Dieter in a whisper. "My dad didn't know or he would have . . ." Dieter rolled his eyes.

"No," said Sasha. "She just made me get up in the morning with Larik."

"She didn't punish you?" questioned Ralph. He couldn't believe it.

"Believe me," said Sasha. "An early morning with a three-year-old was punishment enough. Raisa told me she already has one baby. And she doesn't need another. She expects me to act like an adult."

Just then, Raisa and George returned to the room. They sat down wearily next to Sasha. "Larik is asleep—finally," Raisa sighed.

"Ralph, will you play for us?" she asked. "I saw that you brought your violin."

Ralph looked shy for a moment. Then he smiled

and retrieved his violin. Sasha stood by the window, enjoying the cool breeze. Ralph tuned his instrument and prepared to play.

Sasha studied his friend. Ralph had a short, round body with stocky legs and arms. His straight dark hair was brushed back from a round, pale face. Somehow his nose and ears didn't quite fit his face. Blue eyes topped with heavy brows were drawn into a serious look of concentration. He began the first light trills with his bow.

Ralph lost himself in the music. Pudgy fingers flew across the strings. Clumsy arms became graceful. His body was controlled as he skillfully directed his bow. His violin sang.

Sasha glanced out the window. Across the street, a couple stopped their evening stroll in the park to enjoy the music.

3

Change of Course

Sasha stretched out one leg and then the other. He willed his muscles to relax in the cool morning air. He tied his track shoes tighter and took off his jacket. A light fog misted in from the Baltic Sea. Soon the sun would emerge.

The other boys on the track team hovered around. They waited for the coach to organize the relay teams.

"Good to see you back," called the coach to Sasha as he walked past. "Did you run during the school break?"

Sasha nodded. Coach smiled back. "Get a few seconds off?"

"I don't know. I didn't have anyone to officially time me," said Sasha.

"I'll time you myself in a few minutes. Do a warm-up lap first," ordered Coach.

"Right," Sasha agreed as he sprinted off.

"Slow down, Bausch. I said warm up!" yelled Coach.

Dieter saw Sasha. He began to jog down the track toward him. "Sasha, wait. I'll run with you," he called.

Sasha did a few wide circles waiting for Dieter to catch up.

"You'll have to run hard this season to catch up with me," Dieter laughed. Now running at full speed, Dieter flew by Sasha.

"Don't worry," said Sasha. "This is my year." Together they raced down the track. They matched stride for stride. Pushing hard, they crossed the finish line together.

Sasha caught his breath for a few moments. Then he wedged his feet into the starting blocks. His fingers balanced on the track and his eyes were glued forward. He felt energy electrify him.

"Go!" shouted Coach. He pressed the stopwatch timer.

Sasha pushed with all his might into an upright stance. He stretched his legs to begin his acceleration. He sucked in all the air his lungs would hold. Sasha surged forward. Arms up and legs pumping, Sasha tore his way down the track. His mind shouted run!

Sasha sprinted around the track once. He stretched out to cross the finish line. Coach pressed his stopwatch.

"Good," said Coach. Sasha began to slow his speed. He turned and trotted back.

"You did take off some time," cheered Coach. "Seven seconds. That's great."

Sasha nodded. He was still waiting for his breathing to slow.

Dieter watched from the side. "Soon you'll be able to beat me," he called.

"He just did," said Coach.

"I can do better," said Sasha after he had caught his breath. "I can still do better at the start."

"You'll have to," said Coach. "You still need to take off at least four seconds. The start is vital in the 400. Have you been working on the longer runs, Sasha?

Sasha groaned. "Yes, I can do the 800-meter run too."

"Your weakness is in the blocks," continued Coach. "If you run a longer race, it becomes less of a problem. I think you have the endurance for the 800-meter. It could be your ticket to the national team.

"It's a more difficult race," Coach explained. "I want you to work on the distance races the rest of the week. Do several miles every morning too. I'll clock you next Monday." He walked off, shouting for the relay to prepare.

Dieter walked over to Sasha. "800!" he exclaimed. "Coach put you on the killer distance. Nobody can do that one right. Well, at least you won't have to compete with me."

Sasha held his tongue.

"Good run, Sasha," called Ralph as he joined them.

"Thanks," puffed Sasha. He watched Dieter position himself for the relay.

"Come on, Sasha. I'll do some laps with you. My race is later," said Ralph.

"Sasha, what are you doing up so early?" asked Raisa. "It's not even light yet."

Sasha bounded down the back stairs. "Good morning," he said. "Coach has me on a morning run. I have to do a few miles before school. I'll be back for breakfast," he called. He closed the back door and trotted down the walk.

Sasha ran through the early morning streets of Riga. A slow trot took him to Freedom Boulevard. By the time he had reached the tall Freedom Monument, he was building into a steady pace. He always ran around the base of the monument three times for good luck.

Early spring flowers bloomed at the base of the memorial. The people of Latvia had built the monument with money from their own pockets. He knew Riga, his adopted city, had been founded in 1201. But in all those years, Latvia had enjoyed true freedom for less than 20 years. Freedom was very new and precious. The people of Latvia would not surrender it easily.

Next, he ran across the trolley tracks to Old Town. Here the cobbled streets dove off in odd directions. They were a jumble of angles. Sasha liked the old, brightly painted buildings.

He ran through the central square. The Dome Cathedral towered above him. The golden roosters perched on top of each church spire foretold the weather. Today the roosters faced toward the sea. That meant fine weather for the day.

This morning, Sasha could hear the huge organ behind the cathedral walls thundering with Bach. The organist liked to practice in the early morning too.

Sasha continued to the port on the Daugava River. As usual, it was choked with cargo ships. The crews began unloading before dawn. They stacked the docks with merchandise.

He followed the river toward the sea. Then Sasha turned inland at the old fortress. Its turrets reminded him of sand castles by the sea. He wound his way past the crumbling medieval wall.

Then he ran through the Swedish Gate. Sasha reached out his hand and brushed the top end of an old cannon. It had been buried in the corner of the gateway long ago. Sasha said a silent prayer for peace.

Finally, he crossed into the park. He ran along the gentle stream that flowed through the city.

Sasha jogged up the steps at home. He hoped breakfast was ready.

4
A Letter

"What do you think of the new chemistry teacher?" Ralph whispered. "I'm already lost."

Ralph shook his head in despair. The boys were eating their lunches by the school gate.

"I'll go over it with you tonight, if you like," said Sasha. "It's just atomic numbers."

"*Just,* you say," moaned Ralph. "He wants us to know all those numbers!"

"You have to," laughed Sasha. "Otherwise, how can you figure the formulas?"

"I'll never make it," moaned Ralph.

Master Heff closed the lab book and asked, "Any questions?"

No one spoke. "Fine. Then complete the next lab assignment for tomorrow," he instructed. A quiet groan echoed through the classroom. The boys left quickly.

"Master Bausch, could I speak to you for a moment?" asked Master Heff as Sasha walked past his desk.

"Yes, sir," said Sasha. He couldn't think of anything he had done wrong.

"Nice job on the last assignment, Bausch. I think you understand chemistry," said his teacher.

"It makes sense to me, sir," agreed Sasha.

"And thank you for helping Master Zimmer," continued Master Heff. He stroked his short, trimmed beard. "I appreciate your efforts to get him through this class. I understand last term was a disaster."

"Well, a teacher can make a big difference in a difficult subject," suggested Sasha.

"Yes, I did hear about poor old Master Porkoff," smiled Master Heff. "Don't worry. I can see quite well."

Raisa looked up as Sasha closed the back door behind him. "Anything to eat?" he asked.

She smiled. "Yes, there are **piroshkis** left from lunch. How was practice?"

Sasha shrugged. "The longer races are much harder. But I seem to be able to get a second wind. I think the coach might be right. I might need to switch to the 800-meter in order to qualify." Sasha stuffed a large bite of meat pastry into his mouth.

Raisa said, "We got a letter."

Sasha turned quickly from wolfing his snack. "From Mama?"

Raisa looked very sad and said, "No, it's from Lazare."

"What did he say? Why hasn't Mama written? I have been so worried," said Sasha.

"I'll let you read it for yourself," whispered Raisa. She handed him the folded sheets.

A Letter

Dear Friends,

Poppy and I send you Stalin's best wishes. You know what a fan Poppy is of our mustached leader. Your mama has had to take another trip out of Moscow. She is going where she was assigned before. She wants you to know that she will be fine. They treat the medical doctors better than the other guests. Please don't worry that this had something to do with last time. Someone at the hospital nominated her for this honor.

My daughter and I are fine. Poppy is staying with us now. Sasha, do you remember the wonderful trip that you and your mother made to Sudzal? Now it is like that across the land. The rooks would not listen, or perhaps they did not care. Now, even the rooks are afraid.

In your last letter, you spoke of school and running track. Your mother is so proud of you. She reminds you not to waste a single day.

Your friend,
Lazare

Raisa said, "Do you understand it, Sasha?"

Sasha stared at the letter. "Mama has been sent back to the **gulag**."

33

Raisa gasped. "I had heard rumors of **purges** everywhere. Many people are being sent to prisons."

Sasha nodded. Swallowing hard, he tried not to cry. "Everyone is afraid. They are turning in anyone they can."

"Who are the *rooks*?" asked Raisa.

"The powerful ones," answered Sasha. "That is what Lazare always called them. He is saying that the starvation is even worse than when I left. I told you about the starving people in the countryside."

"Poor Mama. What a waste. I feel so helpless," said Raisa. Sasha heard the catch in her voice.

"She did say that the last time wasn't so awful for her. Not like it was for Lazare. The gulag almost killed him," Sasha said.

He remembered the skeleton man staring out the door at him. Lazare was an old friend of Sasha's father. He had spent five years in the gulag for expressing his opinions.

"Raisa, Mama wouldn't want you to worry. Perhaps we can contact the Red Cross. Sometimes the packages get through. We could try, anyway," suggested Sasha. He placed his hands on his big sister's shoulders, trying to comfort her.

"Yes," she agreed. "I'll go tomorrow."

5

Easter

The days were getting longer as Easter approached. Sasha looked forward to the celebration. Raisa had told him that they celebrated the holiday in the traditional Russian way.

Raisa hard-boiled eggs for decorating. Sasha showed Larik how to decorate them.

"I'll put the lines on with the hot wax," explained Sasha.

He held the **kistka** over the candle flame. Sasha used the tool to draw wax designs on the egg. The melted wax cooled quickly as Sasha drew delicate lines. He made a spiral, which symbolized protection.

"Now you can drop it in the dye," said Sasha. Larik's chubby hand dropped the egg into the color.

"What color is that?" Raisa asked her son.

"Yellow," answered Larik with confidence.

"That's right," smiled Raisa.

Raisa took the tall **kulich** bread from the oven. Sasha and Larik sniffed the spice-filled air. Raisa noticed the boys' hopeful expressions.

"No, you can't have any," laughed Raisa. As the hot bread cooled, she drizzled sweet lemon icing on it. A tall candle would be added on Easter Sunday.

Sasha woke early on Easter morning. He had promised Raisa he would help carry the food to the church to be blessed.

Sasha carried the ham. Laddy and George carried the special kulich breads. Raisa carried a basket of colorful decorated eggs.

Larik held on to Sasha's coat. Larik carried one yellow egg to be blessed.

The doors of the Orthodox church stood open. Faithful followers came for the blessing. Eight round domes topped the church. Each raised a golden cross to the blue sky.

Sasha liked studying the brightly painted interior. Solemn-looking saints covered the walls and arches. Gold-framed portraits surrounded the altar.

After the dazzling spring sunshine, Sasha blinked in the gloom. Dim light peeked through rainbow glass. The air hung thick with incense in the ancient church. It tickled Sasha's nose.

The priests received the foods to be blessed. They wore fine brocade robes. Their tall hats glittered in the light. They blessed the food with a giant crucifix.

Sasha waited at the back with Larik. Laddy and George helped Raisa collect the feast. Larik carried his egg home.

As they opened the door to their home, Raisa said, "Please take Larik for me, will you, Sasha? The guests will be arriving soon. I have to prepare the dining room."

Sasha nodded. He lifted Larik onto his back. "Come on, my friend," Sasha said. "Time to go out in the garden for a bit. Are there some flowers we could pick for your mama today?"

Larik nodded. "Yellow ones in the garden," agreed Larik.

"Yes. Let's go pick them. Your mama will like that," said Sasha.

The boys returned with handfuls of narcissus as an offering for the Easter table.

"Oh, my darling. They are beautiful," Raisa said to Larik. She held the brilliant blossoms to her face. She breathed in their fresh fragrance.

"I didn't let him pick them all," said Sasha.

"Thank you, Sasha," said Raisa. She smiled and kissed him on the cheek. "Happy Easter."

"We didn't have any of these things for Easter in Moscow," said Sasha. He looked around the room. A baked ham held the place of honor. The sideboard was loaded with a dozen cold dishes. Candle-topped kulichs towered above the other foods.

Raisa nodded. "Mama stopped the traditional celebration when you were very small. Right after the civil war in Russia, it was safe to quietly carry on the old Orthodox traditions. But then, even those were banned. Mama always felt it was best to carry her faith inside rather than show it to others."

Raisa continued, "I remember these things from when I was very young. Poppy used to make kulich and **paskha**. I remember dying the eggs with you when you were not much bigger than Larik. The rest I

38

have learned from the Russian community here in Riga. The old women are a wealth of information. I've decided to keep the old ways."

"George doesn't mind?" asked Sasha.

"No. We observe Latvian customs as well. It is so strange to me that two countries so close together should have such different traditions." She smiled. "But this way, Larik will know both ways."

"It's a great way to get more holidays," chimed in Laddy. He snitched a bite of ham off the tray.

Sasha studied the Russian treats. It had been a long time since he'd had paskha. He remembered the taste of the sweet creamy cheese. His stomach rumbled in anticipation of the feast to come.

There was a knock at the door. Sasha opened it to admit a large group of the neighbors.

"Happy Easter!" they announced. They had come to feast. Then they would go on to the next house and feast some more.

It was a day of joyful celebration. Larik showed his yellow egg to all the guests. And Sasha enjoyed his traditional Russian Easter.

6
The Joke

"Come on, Sasha. It's just a little harmless joke," pleaded Dieter.

"I really don't want to do it, Dieter," said Sasha. "Master Heff is new to Riga. He is trying to become a part of the **gymnasium**. I don't think we should torture him like some poor first-year boy."

"He's just a Russian immigrant," Dieter pointed out.

Sasha felt chilled. He looked up and said, "I'm just a Russian immigrant."

Dieter looked surprised for a moment. Then he looked away.

Ralph chimed in. "It's not going to hurt anyone, Sasha. Look at it this way. If we're lucky, it will make a big mess. Then we won't have time for the quiz Heff wants us to take. Then you can help me tonight. Maybe I'll be able to pass by tomorrow. You're just helping a friend."

"You don't have to do anything," said Dieter. "Just ask Heff a question at the beginning of class. Then I can switch the chemicals."

Sasha looked skeptical.

Dieter explained, "I found a discarded sodium chloride container in the trash. Heff won't suspect a thing. I'll do the hard part." Dieter held up a small metal can.

Sasha searched his mind for a way out. He couldn't find one.

"What do I ask him?" he asked finally.

"It doesn't matter," encouraged Dieter. "Pretend you don't understand the last question on the lab. Just keep him busy for a moment. I have everything all ready to switch. He'll never know it was any of us. Trust me."

The three boys stood outside the door to the chemistry lab. The door swung open. The previous class spilled into the hall. The familiar harsh smell of the chemistry lab greeted Sasha's nose.

"What's in the can?" Sasha asked Dieter as they entered.

"Sodium," Dieter whispered in Sasha's ear.

Dieter went in with Ralph. They stood near the front of the room. They pretended to be deep in conversation.

Nearby, Master Heff was busy preparing the chemicals and tools for the next class. He paid little attention to the boys.

Sasha took a deep breath. He walked into the room. "Uh, Master Heff?"

Master Heff looked up from his notes. He smiled at Sasha.

"How are you today, Master Bausch? Did you have a good Easter?" the teacher asked. He pushed his small gold spectacles up to rest on the bridge of his nose.

"Uh, yes, sir. And you, sir?" asked Sasha. The sweat dripped down the back of his collar. His ears burned. He knew they were as red as beets.

"Well, it wasn't like the old days," continued Master Heff. There was just a hint of a sigh. "Of course, I don't have my family here with me. But some neighbors, a Russian family, invited me to dinner. It was very nice to celebrate in the old way."

Sasha asked, "Where is your family, sir?"

Master Heff stared past Sasha into space. "They were sent to Siberia almost ten years ago. I never heard from them again. I don't know where my mother, father, or little sister are. I was away at school when the **Cheka** came to our farm. The police said we were **kulaks**. That means . . ."

"I know what *kulak* means," whispered Sasha.

Master Heff nodded. He continued, "My family was forced from our home. My uncle came and took me from school that night. He brought me to Latvia the next day. I suppose he saved my life."

Sasha couldn't speak. He stared at the stricken face of his teacher. Sasha understood the man's feelings.

Out of the corner of his eye, Sasha saw Dieter replacing the metal container of chemicals. Sasha tried to signal Dieter not to do it. Then he looked at Ralph, pleading with his eyes for them to forget the joke.

Dieter smiled wickedly. He signaled that the job was complete. The bell rang and Master Heff ordered the students to take their places. It was too late for Sasha to grab the can himself. Master Heff would see. There was nothing he could do but sit down.

He didn't know how to tell Master Heff that something bad would happen. He didn't want to get his best friends in trouble. Dieter and Ralph had been the boys who had befriended Sasha when he was new at school. Back then, he could hardly keep up with the German everyone spoke. How could he get his friends into trouble?

Master Heff brought the class to order. "In a moment, we will take the quiz I told you about yesterday. But first I would like to review compounds and mixtures. Who can tell me the difference?"

Sasha looked at the floor. He couldn't think. Another boy answered the question correctly.

"Do you all understand the difference?" asked Master Heff.

"Master Zimmer, how about you?"

Ralph stood next to his seat. Straight-faced, he said, "Yes, sir. I'm prepared to take the quiz."

Master Heff nodded as Ralph sat down. Sasha saw the smirk on Dieter's face.

Master Heff took a large beaker of water from his worktable. "Now, I'm going to combine water and sodium chloride. What will that be—a compound or a mixture?" Master Heff picked up Dieter's canister.

Sasha continued to stare at the floor. He saw Master Heff add the wrong chemical to the water. He stood and shouted, "No!"

But no one heard him. Sasha knew that even a tiny amount of sodium added to water would explode. A handful hit the water, and the noise was deafening.

The Joke

Master Heff dropped the beaker of water. It continued exploding onto the tabletop and floor. Boys shouted and began to drop to the ground by their desks. Ones near the door tried to escape in a panic.

It was all over in a moment. Master Heff hadn't moved. His glasses had slipped off his face. His lab coat dripped water and several chemicals that had not survived the blast. Thin silvery smoke hung in the air. A stench filled the classroom.

A defeated look settled on the teacher's face. "Class is dismissed for the day," he said quietly.

Sasha slipped out the door of the classroom. He was too embarrassed to offer to help Master Heff clean up. He knew he would betray his involvement in the prank if he spoke to him now.

Several boys were talking loudly.

"Did you see his face?"

"I was so surprised. It scared me to death."

"What did he mix together? Did he know that would happen?"

Sasha left the hall. He joined Dieter and Ralph by the school gate.

"You did that perfectly, Sasha," laughed Dieter. "He didn't see a thing. Did you see his face when he dropped the beaker? I almost died laughing."

"That was great, Dieter. That was the best joke yet," howled Ralph.

Sasha just walked past them. He couldn't face anyone.

"What's the matter, Sasha?" Ralph asked.

"Nothing," growled Sasha.

7

Confession

Sasha skipped track practice. The thought of running in the fresh spring air made him sick to his stomach. A smoky smell clung to his clothes and his conscience.

He hid out in his room until dinner. Raisa sent Larik up to call him to the meal.

Larik was barely able to open the door. "Time to eat, Sasha," he called from the doorway. "Sasha, time to eat." He moved into the room.

"Not now, Larik. I'll come later," said Sasha. He buried his face in his pillow.

"Mama says come down now," insisted the little boy. He pulled on Sasha's hand.

"I'm not hungry!" shouted Sasha.

Larik looked frightened and ran back down the stairs.

"Wonderful," said Sasha to himself. "Now I'm bullying three-year-olds."

Sasha got to his feet wearily and dragged himself down the stairs. He walked into the dining room. Larik hid behind his mother's skirt.

"I'm sorry, Larik," apologized Sasha. "I'm sorry I was grumpy. Come on. I'll let you sit next to me."

Larik looked skeptical.

"I'll share my dessert with you," Sasha bribed the little boy. "Come on, give me a big hug. Uncle Sasha is feeling very sad tonight."

The little boy squeezed Sasha around the knees.

Sasha patted the boy's blond hair. It was as soft as kitten fur. "Thanks, Larik. I need forgiveness."

"One for now and one for later," said Larik as he hugged Sasha again.

Sasha didn't eat much at dinner.

"Aren't you feeling well, Sasha?" asked Raisa. "I noticed you came home early. Do you feel ill?" She touched Sasha's brow with her cool hand.

"I'm all right," sighed Sasha.

"Did something happen at school?" asked George.

"No," lied Sasha. "Nothing happened. I'm just tired, I guess." His ears burned.

"Are your friends coming over tonight?" asked Raisa as she gave Larik his dinner.

"No, I think I just want to spend the evening alone," said Sasha. "I'm going to bed early."

After dinner, Sasha retreated to his room. He lay on his bed, staring at the ceiling. He wondered where his mother was right now. Could she be taking care of Master Heff's little sister or father? Sasha wondered if any of them were still alive. Loneliness lay on his chest like a stone.

Sasha stared into the darkness all night. The hours dragged by painfully. Sasha turned restlessly in his bed. Sometimes he left his bed and stared out his window at the deserted street below.

As the sun rose, he put on his running clothes. He left through the back door, not allowing it to slam. He went out into the cool, damp air.

A fog had risen off the Baltic. The smell of the sea wafted through the quiet streets. Sasha didn't pay any attention to where he ran. He just ran—trying to clear his jumbled thoughts.

He found himself at the school gates. He remembered that some of the teachers had rooms in the old apartment house across the street. He jogged over and looked for Master Heff's name.

Sasha scanned the dozen yellowing name cards by the door. *Heff*—a new white card stood out.

Sasha waited on the front step. The sun rose higher. The fog began to lift. Thin streaks of blue could be seen through the gray haze. The sun sifted its way through the layers of moisture to warm Sasha's shoulders.

Finally, Sasha stood and rang the bell next to the new name card. After a moment, the front door unlatched. Sasha walked into the dim hall. It smelled of boiled cabbage and old socks. The walls were painted muddy brown. The floors held layers of dirty footprints. He walked up the steps, noticing the worn carpet. It was so thin that he could see the wood treads underneath.

Sasha knocked on the third door in the hall—number six. Master Heff opened the door. He looked surprised to see Sasha.

"Master Bausch. This is an early surprise," he said.

"I . . . I hope I didn't wake you, sir," said Sasha. He didn't know what to say next.

Master Heff studied Sasha's worried face. He swung the door open a little wider. "Why don't you come in and have a cup of tea with me? I was just about to fix myself a little breakfast."

Sasha nodded and entered.

"I don't go down for meals except in the evening," continued the teacher. "The lady of the house doesn't mind if I make tea in the mornings."

Sasha suddenly felt very cold. "Thank you, sir. I'd like some tea."

"Good," said Master Heff. He went over to a small table by the window. It held a brass **samovar** and two glasses.

"Do you like sugar with your tea?" he asked with his back to Sasha. "My grandfather taught me the old way to drink tea—the Russian way."

Sasha smiled. He hadn't had a sugar cube with his tea since he had left Moscow. Poppy, his nanny, had always kept sugar on the kitchen table. Sasha remembered popping a lump into his mouth and then sucking in hot tea.

"Yes, please, sir. My mother didn't like me to use poor manners. But it was fun. And it didn't hurt anything," said Sasha.

Master Heff studied Sasha. He poured the strong tea from the tiny teapot on top of the samovar. Then he filled the glass with steaming water from the spigot at the bottom. The glass was placed in its brass holder before Sasha.

Master Heff seated himself in the other chair. He began to stir his tea with a small silver spoon.

"No, it didn't hurt anyone, did it?" he said.

Sasha realized that Master Heff wasn't talking about the sugar anymore.

"I . . . I'm sorry, sir," said Sasha. He pulled the rickety chair out to sit down. "I feel bad about yesterday. I didn't think it up, but I did participate."

"I figured that," said the teacher. "You were supposed to distract me. Am I right?"

"Yes," said Sasha miserably. "Only I didn't know you were going to tell me about your family. I hoped my friends wouldn't go through with it. But I guess I knew they would. I just didn't want to let them down, either. They befriended me when I came to Riga." Sasha shook his head. He sipped the hot tea.

"They don't mean any harm. They just like to play these stupid tricks. I came to tell you that I'm sorry for my part. I'll do anything you want to make it right. I could grade papers for you or clean up after school," Sasha offered.

"You have track, don't you?" asked Master Heff. "I have seen you out running before and after school."

"Yes, sir. But I need to pay you this debt," continued Sasha. "I'll run earlier."

Master Heff smiled. "No, that isn't necessary. I think you have already paid the debt with a sleepless night. Will you tell me who your fellow troublemakers were?"

Sasha stared at his tea. "I can't do that, sir. They're my friends."

"Hmm . . . yes, well. I have an idea of who it was, anyway. You see, teachers were once boys too. Most of us have done our share of pulling pranks ourselves." Master Heff smiled to himself.

He leaned forward and said, "I pulled a really good one on my math teacher once. She never did find out who put the alum in her tea."

"Alum!" cried Sasha. "You did that? That stuff tastes awful."

"I know," he laughed. "You should have seen her face." Master Heff puckered his lips and squinted his eyes.

Sasha smiled and sipped his tea. He debated with himself whether to continue.

"My family is Russian too," blurted Sasha. "My mother is still in Moscow. We haven't heard from her in three months."

The smile faded on Master Heff's face. "You are Russian?" he asked. "I didn't realize that. Your name is more German than Russian. And your accent is good. Would you mind if we speak in Russian? I can think more quickly that way," said Master Heff, slipping into Russian.

Sasha nodded. It felt comfortable to speak in his native language.

"I was born in Moscow," Sasha explained. "I came to Latvia when I was 12. My mother smuggled me out. I came with my **babushka** and my poppop. Mama spent a year in the gulag because of the trick she played on the emigration officials. Now we hear that she has been taken again. I'm so worried about her. She has no one to protect her."

"And who protects you?" asked Master Heff.

Sasha shrugged his shoulders. "My father died two years ago. He had been ill for a long time. Poppop lived only a short time after we came to Latvia. Babushka died this year. Now I live with my older sister and her husband.

"I'm fine," continued Sasha. "I'm just so worried about my mother. We've only had one short note from a friend."

"I do have a few people that might help," Master Heff considered. He pulled on his mustache. "Let me make a few inquiries. Perhaps I can find out something. I have spent many years looking for my family. I may have more success helping yours."

Master Heff fell silent for a moment. Then he said, "Let me show you something."

The teacher rose from his creaky chair. He began to search through a drawer in his battered wardrobe.

"Here it is," he said finally. He placed a small tissue-wrapped bundle on the table in front of Sasha.

"Go ahead and look," urged Master Heff. The teacher pointed to the yellowing paper. Sasha carefully unwrapped the package to find an old linen handkerchief. Many names had been carefully embroidered into the cloth. Each was a different color.

"They look like people's signatures!" exclaimed Sasha. He gently turned the cloth in his hand and raised it to the light.

"Yes. I have had that one for several years," explained Master Heff. "A woman stitched the names of inmates at the gulag to remember them. She was fortunate enough to be released. She told others about those who were still held. Those names are the people who were in her cell."

Sasha traced the names with his finger. He thought of the people imprisoned in the gulag. He felt sorry for them and their families.

"There are many little secrets to helping those who are held. I will try to contact someone near your mother," promised the teacher.

"Thank you, sir. I would very much appreciate it. I need to go home now. There is school today," said Sasha.

Sasha took a final noisy slurp of tea. Then he crunched the sweet sugar.

"See you in class," said Master Heff. Then the teacher added with a smile, "And no more tricks."

8

Into the Storm

Ralph and Dieter met Sasha in the hall that morning. Sasha squared his shoulders and said, "I went to see Master Heff."

"You told?" gasped Ralph. He looked frightened. Wide blue eyes accented his pale face.

Dieter rolled his eyes.

"I wouldn't tell on you. You should know that," said Sasha. "I did tell Master Heff what my part was. I apologized to him for what I did."

"Wonderful!" moaned Dieter. "He'll find out we're friends. Then we'll be in trouble too."

"I don't think this will go any further. And I won't give your names," repeated Sasha. "But I think you two should go in and admit what you did."

"My father would kill me if he knew what happened," hissed Ralph.

Sasha shook his head. "Did you at least study and make this all worthwhile?"

Ralph smiled weakly. "Not really. I knew you were upset with us. I was afraid to come over to your house. You should have seen your face when you left yesterday."

Dieter said, "Come on. If we don't look guilty, we can still get away with it."

Dieter opened the door to the chemistry lab. He gave Master Heff a wide, innocent smile. "Morning, sir."

"Good morning, Dieter. You too, Ralph. Are you still ready for our little quiz?" asked Master Heff.

"Yes," Ralph mumbled. He looked at the floor.

"Good morning, Sasha. Could I speak to you for a moment? Outside, please," said Master Heff. His face looked very stern.

The door closed behind them. Master Heff said, "Unfortunately, the headmaster heard about the explosion. I guess it was the talk of the school. Sasha, someone has come forward. They named you in the prank. I didn't give your name. I promise."

Master Heff looked very worried. "I don't want you to be expelled over this. It just isn't worth that."

Sasha felt a cold hollowness in his stomach. He tried to swallow. A sour taste filled his mouth.

"Do I need to go see the headmaster?" Sasha asked.

Master Heff nodded. "He's waiting for you."

Sasha walked down the corridor to the school's central staircase. His feet were heavy with fear. Sasha climbed to the top floor. He counted the steps.

"Please don't tell Raisa. Please don't tell my sister," he prayed under his breath. Somehow he had to persuade the headmaster not to tell his sister. Raisa had enough to worry about as it was.

Sasha knocked. He opened the heavy door to the headmaster's office. "You asked to see me, sir," said Sasha timidly.

The headmaster looked up. He silently motioned Sasha into the room. This was the first time Sasha had been to Headmaster Fleishman's office.

Sasha looked around at the beautiful old paneling and shelves of leather-bound books. A table in front of the window gleamed. It held silver-framed pictures of a happy family.

Silently, the headmaster pointed to a stiff chair in front of his large desk. Sasha sat. He waited until the headmaster chose to look up again. Sasha concentrated on taking slow, deep breaths.

"Master Bausch," said the headmaster. His voice was deep but quiet. "I would like you to tell me about the incident in the chemistry lab yesterday. You have been accused of causing the explosion."

"Who said that, sir?" asked Sasha. The words stuck in his throat.

"Never mind who," said **Herr** Fleishman. He folded his arms across his ample chest. Sasha studied the gleaming bald spot on the top of Herr Fleishman's head.

"Well, sir," Sasha tried to clear his throat. "I did know that something might happen. But I didn't know how big the explosion would be. I wouldn't have allowed it to happen if I'd known. I distracted Master Heff so that the trick could be played on him. I've apologized to him already. I've taken responsibility for my part."

Sasha paused. "I hope that you don't have to tell my sister," he continued. "She's very concerned about other things right now." Sasha sat in silence.

"Will you tell me the other boys' names?" Herr Fleishman asked.

"No," whispered Sasha.

"Sasha," said the headmaster in a softer tone. "I would like to help you with this. I understand this was just a prank. You must trust me. I would like to think you could come to me and trust me with confidences. I know you don't have a father. I could be a friend to you."

The headmaster smiled, and Sasha relaxed. "Thank you, sir," Sasha said. "I didn't want to hurt Master Heff. He is Russian, like me. I felt terrible when I found out."

"Yes, he is an immigrant, just like you," the headmaster said as he rose from his desk. He walked slowly toward the window. "I don't want you to worry about this for now, Master Bausch. There is a way. Yes, I will take care of everything. Go on back to class."

Relieved, Sasha raced down the steps. Perhaps Raisa would never have to know. Somehow he would find a way to make amends with Master Heff.

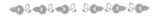

"Did you get expelled?" Ralph's voice quivered.

Sasha leaned on the front gate. He felt weak in the knees. He could only shake his head.

Dieter joined them a moment later. "It was all over school that you went to see Herr Fleishman," he said.

"I didn't get expelled. And I didn't mention either of you," Sasha said.

Dieter eyed Sasha suspiciously. Then he smiled. "I know that. We would have been up to the top floor by now if you had. Come on, you missed practice yesterday. Today is the day I will pull ahead of you again. You know we have that big meet this weekend."

"I'll time you, if you like," suggested Ralph.

9
Winds of Change

Ralph was missing in chemistry the next morning. Sasha waited outside the door of the classroom until the last possible minute. A loud buzzer hummed through the hall.

Maybe Ralph overslept this morning, Sasha thought to himself. Dieter waved as Sasha took his seat by the window. Sasha tried to concentrate on the formula that Master Heff was demonstrating. He kept looking over at Ralph's empty seat.

Finally, the class was dismissed. Sasha saw Ralph walk slowly past the classroom. Ralph's usually pale face looked almost green. His eyes were puffy and red. His shoulders slumped as he slowly shuffled down the hall.

"Ralph, wait," called Sasha. "Where were you?"

"The headmaster's office," moaned Ralph. He never took his eyes off the floor. "Someone said I pulled the trick—by myself. The headmaster has sent me home for the rest of the term. I'm expelled!"

Dieter looked shocked. "Sasha! You said you wouldn't tell."

Sasha turned to Dieter. "I didn't!" he shouted. "I wouldn't do that. Ralph, you know I wouldn't. Don't you?"

"I just know that I have to go home and tell my father I'm not going to graduate this term. This is worse than failing chemistry. I didn't even do anything. But Herr Fleishman wouldn't listen. I told him how awful I am at chemistry. I didn't even know what that powder was," Ralph wailed.

"Sasha, I can't believe you did this to our friend!" cried Dieter. His face was red from anger. "I suppose you will turn me in next."

Sasha stood in the hall. He was unable to speak as his friends walked away.

Then he bounded up the stairs, three at a time. Sasha stood in front of the headmaster's door. He gathered his courage and knocked softly.

"Sir, may I speak to you for a moment?" asked Sasha through a crack in the door.

"Come in, Sasha. What is it?" asked Herr Fleishman.

"I just spoke to Ralph, sir." Sasha tried to catch his breath. "I hoped you might reconsider his punishment."

"I don't think so, Sasha. He did participate in the prank. I was told that he initiated it. That way he wouldn't have to take the quiz," answered Herr Fleishman. He crossed his arms and leaned back in his chair.

"Please, sir. He didn't even know what would happen. Ralph is hopeless with chemistry. He couldn't—" begged Sasha.

The headmaster waved Sasha's argument away. "It is just as well he is gone. We don't want his kind around here, anyway."

Sasha was confused. "His *kind*?" he repeated.

"Yes, you know—Jewish," Herr Fleishman whispered.

Sasha couldn't think of anything to say. He turned around and walked out of the finely paneled room. He softly shut the door behind him.

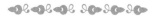

Sasha began his afternoon run. He chose not to stay with the group of other boys running through the narrow streets of Riga. Sasha worked his way to the river and then ran to the port. Huge ships crowded near the pier. Men swarmed over them, unloading cargo.

He watched as a passenger ship edged away from the dock. It was powered by the small tugboats at its side. The ship crept downriver to the Gulf of Riga.

Sasha tried to think about what the headmaster had said. Ralph was his friend—a good friend. Sasha had even celebrated Passover at Ralph's house. And other than chemistry, Ralph was a good student. He did not deserve this.

Without realizing it, Sasha arrived at Ralph's house. He stared at the gleaming brass lion head mounted on the door of Ralph's house. He grabbed the handle and willed himself to bang it against the door.

The distant sound of a violin wafted through the house. Sasha listened as he waited. A few seconds later, the door opened slightly. A pair of watery eyes peered from the crack.

"Could I please speak to Ralph?" Sasha asked the old woman dressed in black.

The old woman shook her head. She turned and began to shut the door.

"Remember me, Grandmere? I'm Ralph's friend Sasha. Please. I need to talk to him. Is he home?" Sasha begged.

The old woman pursed her lips. "He doesn't want to see anyone," she said.

"Please, it's very important," pleaded Sasha.

The violin stopped playing. "Let him in, Grandmere," called Ralph.

"Very well," the old woman replied with a sigh.

She opened the door wider. Sasha entered the darkened hall. Ralph stood in the doorway. Light from the window behind him hid his face.

"What do you want, Sasha?" Ralph spoke quietly and without feeling.

"I came to say how sorry I am about everything," began Sasha. "I want you to know that I didn't mention your name. I would never do that. I don't know how the headmaster knew. Maybe because we're friends. I even went to him and asked that you not be punished." The words poured out of Sasha. He wanted so badly for Ralph to believe him.

Ralph studied Sasha's face as he spoke. "It's all right, Sasha. I know you didn't betray me. I think I know why this has happened. My parents have decided that it is time for a change. Perhaps this is the best thing."

"What do you mean?" asked Sasha.

"My parents have decided that we will emigrate to the United States. My mother has a brother there already. He will help us to settle and get my father a job. I will finish school there," Ralph said.

"But why?" cried Sasha. "Just because of a stupid prank?"

"My father thinks this has very little to do with the prank and more to do with . . ." Ralph hesitated. A clock on the fireplace mantel ticked loudly, filling the silence.

"With being Jewish?" Sasha completed the sentence.

"Yes," whispered Ralph.

"But why should that matter to anyone?" asked Sasha.

"It matters to many people. Things have been happening to us lately—frightening things," whispered Ralph. "My parents have tried to ignore it. But Hitler made open threats in his speech in January.

Now my parents fear that the hatred that has erupted in Germany is spilling into Latvia. They think we will be safer in the United States."

"When will you go?" asked Sasha.

"Mother and I go tonight," answered Ralph. "My father will follow soon. He must try to sell our house. A friend is getting the **visas**. There is a ship leaving at midnight. I am packed to go."

Sasha stepped forward into the light. He offered his hand to Ralph. "I had a friend back in Moscow. His name is Albert. When I moved, his parents wouldn't allow him to write to me. I missed him for a long time. But then you were my friend . . ." Sasha couldn't finish the sentence.

"Thank you, Sasha. I will write to you . . ." Ralph hesitated, unable to continue. Then he grinned and joked, "Maybe you will come to the United States someday. I hear there are many beautiful girls."

Sasha smiled. "Yes, maybe I will."

Sasha waved as Ralph closed the door. Sasha walked down the street. He felt like kicking something. With his hands in his pockets and eyes on the ground, he didn't notice Master Heff walking toward him.

"You look upset, Sasha," Master Heff said.

Sasha jumped at the sound of his voice. "I just can't believe this is happening. Everything was going along just fine. Then all of a sudden, it's a terrible mess," sighed Sasha.

"<u>Yes</u>, it is," replied Master Heff. "Wait here for me, Sasha. I'll only be a moment. Then we can talk."

To Sasha's surprise, Master Heff walked hurriedly up the path to Ralph's front door. He knocked insistently. The door soon opened. Master Heff handed over a large envelope. He exchanged a few words with Ralph's father. Master Heff then turned and joined Sasha by the street.

"*You* got the visas?" asked Sasha.

"Yes," answered Master Heff. "When I heard what had happened at school, I came to speak with Ralph's parents. I helped persuade them to make this move. I know some officials. Ralph's parents were born in the **Ukraine**. So it wasn't difficult to get the visas."

"I just don't understand any of this," said Sasha.

"Hate never seems to make sense, does it, Sasha?" asked Master Heff. "But hate is real, and we must guard against it. We must be careful."

The words left Sasha cold.

Master Heff began to cross the quiet street. He turned and said, "Sasha, don't say anything to anyone about this." And he disappeared into the growing dusk.

10

Poppy

"What's up, Sasha?" Laddy asked as he entered the kitchen. "You look like you lost your best friend."

Sasha shrugged. "I think I'm just nervous about the race next Saturday." Sasha knew he could trust Laddy. But Master Heff had said to tell no one.

"Do you think you're ready?" asked Laddy.

"I'm close. The last time the coach timed me, I had dropped ten seconds on the 800-meter race. That will get me into the finals next month. By then, I just might make it," said Sasha.

Somehow, though, he couldn't feel much enthusiasm. It just wouldn't be as much fun running without Ralph.

A loud knock from the front door echoed through the house. Sasha hurried to answer. A telegram boy stood holding a small yellow envelope. Sasha took it. He handed the boy a small coin.

"Is it bad news?" asked Raisa from the stairs. "I hate telegrams."

Sasha tore into the envelope. He quickly read the brief message and said, "No, Raisa. It's good news. It's from Lazare. Poppy is coming! He finally got her a visa. She will come on the train. She'll arrive Sunday morning at 6:30." Sasha grinned up at his sister.

"That's great," chimed in Laddy as he joined them in the hall. "Now I finally get to meet the famous Poppy."

"Perhaps she will know what has happened to Mama," said Raisa.

"I'll go and get her that morning," volunteered Sasha.

"No," smiled Raisa. "I think we all should."

It was a soft morning, lit by a late-setting moon. The eastern horizon was splashed with red, orange, and pink clouds. Sasha carried Larik to the station. Raisa, George, and Laddy followed.

They stood in the quiet train station. It was not yet busy with the day's travelers.

Sasha thought about his own arrival in Riga when he was 12. He remembered not being able to sleep that night on the train. He had jumped at every noise. He had been afraid that someone would find him and make him return to Moscow.

Babushka and Poppop had nodded off, snoring softly. They had been unaware that someone had made a final attempt to stop their escape from Moscow. Sasha recalled the angry face of the emigration officer.

He also remembered the border guards who had moved noisily through the train in the middle of the night. They had demanded the proper papers. Sasha's grandfather had pulled them from his coat pocket. Sasha had stared at the floor while the visas were reviewed. He had known he must not look frightened.

But the men in uniform had only given Sasha a quick glance. Then they had turned away. As the train chugged into free Latvia, Sasha had finally slept.

He remembered his father waiting for him as the train arrived. He and Raisa had put their arms around Sasha and cried.

Yet his mother had paid dearly for his freedom. She had given up her own freedom to serve time in a gulag. Sasha had not even known she had been taken. Months later, a letter had arrived from Poppy.

Sasha blinked the tears of remembrance away. He heard the train whistle pierce the silence.

Little Larik pranced around. He peeked down the tracks. Sasha held firmly to his hand.

"It's coming! It's coming!" Larik cried. "Sasha, what is a *Poppy*?"

"Not what, Larik. Who. Poppy is a very dear friend of ours. She took care of your mama when she was little. And she took care of me until I came to Riga," explained Sasha. He patted the boy's small head.

"Is she like Babushka?" asked the little boy.

"Yes. You remember Babushka, don't you?" asked Sasha.

"Yes. Babushka went to heaven," said Larik.

"Well, Poppy is here. I think you will like her very much," Sasha assured Larik. "She is warm and soft and smells like cinnamon buns."

The train slowed as it moved into the station. Its great steel wheels squealed. Thick black smoke belched from the stack. As the train cars moved by, Sasha searched for the snowy braids and the soft, friendly face he remembered.

He noticed an ancient conductor helping an old

woman down the steps. She seemed too small to be Poppy. But then Sasha saw her smile, and he knew. Poppy rushed over and put her arms around Sasha. She rested her head on his chest.

"Sasha," was all she could say.

Tearful greetings were exchanged. Larik insisted on holding Poppy's hand as they led her to a waiting cab.

"You don't need to take me in an automobile. I can walk," Poppy insisted.

"No," said Raisa. "Papa would have insisted. We're so glad you are here."

They crowded into the taxi. Sasha asked, "How is Lazare?"

Poppy said, "He is doing fairly well. Lazare was the one who convinced the emigration authorities that I should go. Although, it did hurt my feelings to be called useless. Imagine! Me—useless!"

"Never," laughed Sasha.

Raisa looked back from the front seat of the cab. "Poppy, after you have had a chance to rest, we need to know about Mama. We have been so worried."

Poppy reached forward and patted Raisa's hand. "I'll tell you everything," she promised.

Poppy was properly settled in the room that had once been Babushka's. Sasha and Larik gave her a tour of their home. Raisa prepared tea. She ushered everyone into the living room.

"Raisa, dear," said Poppy. "Quit fussing. I feel like a princess come to visit. Could we just go into the kitchen for our tea? I have so much to tell you. I would feel so much more at home there."

Raisa served tea around the old kitchen table. Then Poppy began her story. She looked at Sasha and took his hand.

"You have grown into the fine man I knew you would, Sasha. We all missed you so much when you came to Latvia. The house was so quiet.

"Your mother was arrested and tried very soon after you left," she explained. "I don't know what they called it—treason, I suppose. But she was sent to the gulag within weeks. That horrible woman from the emigration office was very angry with her."

Sasha remembered the woman's cold smile with a shiver.

Poppy continued, "Lazare and his daughter took me in, you know. They were so kind. We got one letter during that year your mother was gone. I suppose that was good. We knew she was still alive."

Poppy looked at Sasha and said, "She told us when she came home that the gulag was a bleak place. It was built in the country. She took care of the other inmates. Her medical skills were very useful there. She came home very thin, but not like Lazare. She recovered very quickly.

"When she came home, your mama started back at the same hospital. I guess they needed doctors more desperately than ever by then. She worked very hard. They were difficult years."

Poppy paused and took a sip of her tea. "Then last year, a new administrator came to the hospital. He was expected to perform miracles with no funds and overworked people. When he couldn't, he started naming doctors as traitors."

"We heard about the purges," said Raisa.

Poppy looked out the window for a moment. Her lip trembled. "I was home when they came for her. The guards always come and wake you at night. She only had a few moments to pack. We heard nothing for more than a month. Then Lazare finally talked to someone who had seen her. She is back at the same gulag as before. We don't know how long she will be held."

Raisa stood and hugged Poppy's shoulders. "Thank you, Poppy. At least we know where she is. I may be able to get a letter through. We're so glad you're here."

Poppy stood. She looked around the kitchen and said, "I will start lunch now."

"Poppy," objected Sasha. "You are our guest."

"No," said Poppy, pulling herself up. She smoothed her almost white hair back into its knot. "I have always earned my keep. They may think I am useless in Russia, but I'm not. Please, can I stay with you and earn my keep?"

Raisa smiled. "I would be very glad for the help, Poppy. Thank you."

11
Trial Run

Sasha shook his arms and legs. He was trying to keep his muscles loose. His race was up next.

"Sasha," said Coach. "This is not a critical race for you. Remember, you are just trying out the 800. Get a feel for the competition. Your times in practice have been good. But remember, you can't just sprint. This race takes thinking and timing. You have to know how much you have left and how much everyone else in the race has put out. Good luck."

Sasha took his place in the third lane. The runners were staggered. In this race, they did not use starting blocks. He filled his lungs with oxygen in deep breaths. He was poised in a ready position as the gun rang in his ears.

Then he was running. Sasha stretched his long legs into a quick pace. Soon he overtook two runners.

The racers were allowed to leave their lanes. Sasha vied for a position on the inside of the track. Then a faster boy jumped ahead of him. He forced Sasha to an outside lane.

Sasha finished the first lap. Only two boys were ahead of him. He was running hard but still feeling fine. Matching pace with another runner, he went into the next turn. Sasha held his ground. He forced the other runner to take the second lane.

Sasha settled in for the long, grueling second lap. He ran with everything in him. Would the race ever end? His lungs had forgotten how to breathe. His legs screamed in agony. His arms felt like 100-pound weights.

He still had 200 meters to go. One runner passed

him. Sasha could only glance to the side. There was nothing he could do. Then another runner took his final sprint. He easily overtook Sasha.

Sasha prayed he would stay on his feet. Ahead, the leader broke joyously through the yellow tape. The crowd cheered. The last runner moved ahead of Sasha just steps before the finish line.

Sasha threw himself over the line and collapsed onto the sideline grass. Stars swam in front of his eyes. His stomach lurched. Painfully, his breath returned.

"Last," he moaned when he could.

Coach walked over after Sasha had a moment to recover. He offered Sasha a hand up. They walked back to the team bench.

"Believe it or not, Sasha, that was a good first try," Coach said.

Sasha just shook his head. He slumped down onto the bench.

"That was just awful," groaned Sasha. He buried his face in his hands. "I didn't have anything left."

"Remember, Sasha," advised Coach. "This is a thinking race. You must know when to run."

For a moment, Sasha didn't have the breath to agree. Then he said, "I'll get it."

"I know," agreed Coach.

12
A Suggestion

Sasha joined Raisa and George in the shade of the beech tree. Its new leaves offered a dappled shade. The garden was a deep green in the early spring's warmth. Bees hummed in the flowers.

Larik dug in the dirt by his mother's feet. Glasses of cool lemonade stood on a tilting wooden table. They dripped condensation into puddles at their bases.

George folded the newspaper. He scowled at the news. Raisa, sensing her husband's mood, asked, "More bad news from Germany?"

"Hitler has threatened Poland again," responded George. "There seems to be no stopping him. England is afraid to move. **Chamberlain** still hesitates."

"They are afraid of another world war," commented Raisa. She bent to stroke her son's silky hair.

"Mama, look," ordered Larik. "I built a fort. And here is the moat."

"That's what we need," sighed Raisa. "A moat around Latvia."

"It would have to be a very deep one to keep Hitler out," said Sasha.

"Sasha, I spoke to someone the other day about visas," began Raisa hesitantly.

"Visas? Who needs a visa?" asked Sasha.

"I found out that it is very simple for a Russian in Latvia to get a visa to go to America." Raisa ignored Sasha's question. "There is something called a *quota*. It allows a certain number of Russians to emigrate to the United States. Very few Russians are being allowed to emigrate from Russia now. So you will have an easier time getting a visa here."

"I don't understand," said Sasha.

"I just want you to think about this, Sasha," Raisa pleaded. "I want you to think about going to America."

A Suggestion

"America!" Sasha was astounded.

"There will be a war in Europe," continued his sister. "Latvia stands between two giants. One or the other will swallow us up. I want you away from it. I have thought about this very carefully. I know it is what Mama would want. You could go to America. You could continue your education there."

"Could we all go? Like Ralph's family?" asked Sasha. "You are Russian too."

"I could go, but not George or Larik," explained Raisa. "It is almost impossible for a Latvian to qualify for a visa right now. You are the only one free to go. We could send you to Papa's cousin in New York."

Sasha's throat felt dry and tight. He tried to swallow a sip of lemonade. He rolled the cool glass between his hands.

"I don't want to leave my family behind again," said Sasha. "You and George and Poppy and Larik are all I have left. How could I turn my back on you?"

"It would just be for a few years—until you're finished with your schooling. Then you could come home," suggested Raisa. Her eyes pleaded.

Sasha stood, carefully setting his glass down. "No," he said. He turned to walk toward the house. The door slammed behind him.

13

Riding Out the Storm

"Come on. Let's go!" shouted Laddy.

"Go where?" moaned Sasha, opening one eye. Sasha tried to focus on the clock by his bedside.

Sasha objected loudly as Laddy pulled back his warm covers. "Laddy, are you crazy? It's five in the morning. This is the first morning in weeks I can sleep late," said Sasha.

"Exactly," cheered Laddy. "I haven't had my first mate to sail with in too long. This is a perfect morning. Don't waste it sleeping. Come on, Sasha."

Sasha put a pillow over his head. But Laddy didn't give up.

"I'm leaving in ten minutes, my friend. Don't miss the boat," he called. He shut the door, leaving Sasha in peace.

Ten minutes later, Sasha stood at the front door waiting for Laddy.

"Hurry up," Sasha said. Laddy smiled as they left the house.

They walked through the early morning streets to the dock near the river's edge. The cobbled streets glistened with morning dew.

They prepared the boat quickly. Soon, the sail caught the light dawn breeze. Sasha held the rudder and studied the city skyline.

The golden roosters on top of the triple steeple of St. Peter's faced the sea. It would be a fine day. A bargeman whistled a "good morning" toot as the boys sailed downriver into the gulf.

"I thought we could do a morning run down the Daugava before there are too many others on the water," Laddy suggested into the wind.

"Aye, aye, captain," replied Sasha.

They moored the boat at Jurmula. It was a small

seaside fishing village. Sasha tied the boat to one of the piers jutting out of the black water. They leaped from the boat onto the weathered planks of the dock.

"Come on," said Laddy. "I heard about a place you might like."

"Where?" asked Sasha.

"Up here, around the bend. A friend told me about it. Just wait and see," promised Laddy.

They walked up the rocky shore, scrambling over moss-covered boulders. Beaches of fine sand lay among the rocks. Mussels clung to the rocks' undersides. The strong, salty smell of the sea washed over Sasha. Pines crept close to the shore, trying to get their roots wet.

"Raisa wants me to go to America," blurted Sasha after a long silence.

"I know," responded Laddy. "She and George spoke to me last night. I heard you weren't too excited about the idea."

"Humph," replied Sasha.

"I guess that's putting it mildly," grinned Laddy.

Sasha had to smile. Then he spoke earnestly, "I have done this before, Laddy. Moving to a new place with your family is hard enough. Moving to a new country where you don't know anyone must be worse."

"I suppose you're right," agreed Laddy.

"The problem is leaving all of you behind. How can I do that?" asked Sasha.

"It would be very difficult," Laddy sympathized.

"And I don't speak English," continued Sasha.

"Yes, that's true," nodded Laddy.

"And we don't know that Hitler will really invade," added Sasha.

"I suppose he could decide that Czechoslovakia and Austria are enough to rule for a while. He could be just bluffing about Poland," concluded Laddy.

"I feel safe here, Laddy!" cried Sasha.

"Yes, for the moment, you are perfectly safe," Laddy said. He looked out over the quiet sea.

"And what about running?" protested Sasha.

"I'm sure they run in America," said Laddy.

Sasha stopped in his tracks and stared at Laddy. "You think I should go too. Don't you?" he asked, shocked.

Laddy smiled kindly at Sasha. Then he sat down on the nearest rock. Suddenly, his face looked deeply sad.

Laddy spoke seriously, "Sasha, in the next few years, the world as we know it is going to fall apart. I can't tell you the exact day that will happen. But I am very sure it will. If you stay here, you will be caught up in it. You will be draft age soon. You will be forced into someone's army to fight someone's battles. The chances of surviving will be slim at best."

Sasha wished he could close his ears and block out Laddy's words.

But Laddy continued. "If you go to America, you will be farther away from the worst of it. You can get your education instead of wasting your life bleeding to death on a battlefield. You can become something. That is what Raisa wants for you. That is all any of us wants. If you do go, you go for all of us. And there is the chance that once you are there, perhaps you can get Larik out."

Sasha stared out at the blue-green sea. Laddy bent down and picked up a sea-smoothed amber stone from the wet sand. He held the golden stone up to the morning light. He turned it slowly in his fingers.

"You see this little creature trapped in the amber?" asked Laddy. He handed it to Sasha.

"He can't fly anymore or taste the nectar of a flower," Laddy said. "His freedom is gone. I'm afraid that's how people in Latvia will feel soon. War will trap us all," Laddy predicted.

Sasha stared at the tiny trapped creature. Then, angrily, he flung it back into the sea.

"I'll think about it," whispered Sasha.

14

Confrontations

Sasha pulled his hands from the bucket of hot, soapy water. He swished through the suds searching for hidden test tubes. None remained. He dumped the gray water down the sink and shook out the scrub brush. He hung up the drippy rubber gloves to dry.

Master Heff raised his head. "Finished?" he asked.

"Yes, sir," replied Sasha. "That sulfur compound sure stinks." Sasha wrinkled his nose.

"Do you feel better now?" Master Heff smiled.

"I'll help tomorrow too," said Sasha.

Master Heff shrugged. "You don't have to, you know. But I can always use the help and the company."

Sasha began to gather his books.

"Have you heard anything about your mother yet?" asked the teacher.

"Oh, I didn't tell you about Poppy," said Sasha. "Poppy is my old nanny. She just came from Moscow. She knows where my mother is being held. My sister is trying to send a letter."

"Well, that is a big step," said Master Heff. He dug through the pocket of his rumpled jacket. He handed Sasha a small slip of paper. "There are people who can help with sending food and medicine."

"Thanks," said Sasha. He turned to go and then stopped.

"Master Heff, why did Ralph get punished?" he asked. "Why are his parents so afraid? Latvia is not like Russia or Germany. There have been no demonstrations here. There isn't any killing."

Master Heff set down the notebook he had been grading. He took off his wire-rimmed reading glasses and rubbed his eyes.

Then he said, "You know about prejudice, Sasha. You can't pretend it doesn't exist. Unfortunately, it's here. It's just not showing it's ugly face clearly yet. But it won't go away."

"My family wants me to leave Latvia," Sasha complained. "They want me to emigrate to America."

"What do you want?" asked Master Heff.

"I want to run and go to university. Yet it seems like hate is spilling all around me. I can't stop it. No one can stop it," said Sasha angrily.

"I don't have any answers," whispered Master Heff sadly.

Sasha wandered toward the front door of the gymnasium. He almost collided with Headmaster Fleishman, who was hurrying out also.

"Oh, excuse me, sir," said Sasha. "I didn't see you."

"Oh, Sasha, it's you. How have you been? How is your family?" asked the headmaster. He was beaming.

"Fine, sir," said Sasha. He stared at the floor.

"Master Heff says you do well in your chemistry class. And the rest of your teachers foresee great things for you. I hear you have been accepted at the university in France. That's good. Perhaps you would like to come up and see me tomorrow? I would like to speak to you about something very important."

The headmaster's eyes glittered. He came very close to Sasha and whispered, "There are some people I would like you to meet."

91

Sasha backed away. He wished he could think of a reason to refuse the invitation. "Uh, yes, sir," he finally replied.

"Good, good. See you tomorrow—about this time," called Fleishman. He hurried through the door and disappeared.

Sasha headed to track practice. Dieter was tying his shoes as Sasha arrived on the track.

"Hello, Dieter. How is practice going?" asked Sasha hesitantly.

Dieter ignored Sasha's question. "You're late," he accused.

"I had some things to do. Coach knew I was coming late." Sasha threw down his bag.

"You did well on Saturday in the relay. Congratulations," offered Sasha.

"Thanks," responded Dieter shyly. Then he continued, "I know you had a tough race Saturday, but you really held on. I don't think I could do that race at all."

Sasha hesitated a moment. Then he asked, "Do you want to run together today? Coach wants me to work on my ending sprint. Could you help me?"

Dieter continued to stare out over the playing field. He seemed unable to look at Sasha. After a long moment, he said, "Sure, why not."

Dieter began to run alongside Sasha. For a while,

they just ran silently, matching pace with each other stride for stride.

Then Dieter stopped suddenly. He said, "I know you didn't tell."

Sasha held out his hand in friendship.

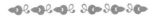

Sasha checked the clock on the wall as he hung up the rubber gloves. He gathered his things and turned out the classroom light. Master Heff had already left. At the top of the staircase, he rapped on the headmaster's door.

Herr Fleishman opened the door. He smiled at Sasha. "Come in. Come in, son," beamed the man. "I am just having some afternoon tea. Such a good custom the English have. Don't you think?"

Sasha joined the man at the table. Small cakes and sandwiches were stacked on a three-tiered plate. An English teapot steamed on a silver tray.

The headmaster poured milk and then tea into Sasha's china cup. Sasha grimaced at the pale liquid but politely took a sip.

"Good?" inquired the older man.

"Yes," said Sasha, a bit surprised. He bit into a sandwich and relaxed. "It's very nice of you to invite me, headmaster."

The man grinned at him. "I would like to look out for you, Sasha. I was once like you, you know. I was a good student, but quiet. I, too, only had a few friends. I would like to see you succeed."

The headmaster bit into a tiny tart. Ruby jam dripped on to his chin. He laughed as he caught the jam with a snowy napkin.

Then Headmaster Fleishman studied Sasha seriously. "I know people that could help you— powerful people."

"Sir?" Sasha was now totally confused.

"You know, Sasha. I could help you get along in the world," offered Herr Fleishman. "I could help you join the right battalion. And help you find the right job after your education.

"You are a very bright boy. You will be very useful after you have completed your education. You're planning to study science, right? Chemistry? Am I correct?" asked Herr Fleishman.

Sasha was speechless. He just stared at the man.

The headmaster rose and looked out the window. "Change is coming, my son. Very big change. We must be ready for it. We must be on the right side, so to speak."

Then he laughed. "You know, that really was very clever. I never would have thought to put sodium in old Heff's beaker."

Confrontations

Sasha was out the door and down the steps before the headmaster turned around. He banged through the front doors of the gymnasium and out the tall iron gate. He ran down the crowded evening streets, dodging little old ladies and couples holding hands. He outran the little green streetcar that would have taken him directly to his destination.

Sasha ran past the monument in the center of Riga. Then, turning back, he slowly ran three times around the woman with upraised arms. He stared up at her. She held shining golden stars in her hands. Then he ran on.

Sasha banged on the wooden door. He kept banging even after he heard Dieter calling from inside, "I'm coming. I'm coming."

Dieter opened the door. Sasha grabbed him by the shirt and pulled him down the front steps.

"Hey, Sasha! Stop! Ow!" cried Dieter.

"How could you?" screamed Sasha. "How could you? I ought to—"

"What is it? What did I do? Have you gone crazy?" hollered Dieter. He freed himself from Sasha's grip and backed away.

"You set Ralph up, didn't you? You did it!" yelled Sasha.

Suddenly Sasha's anger was spent. He sat down on the steps and took a calming breath. "How could you do that to our friend?"

"How did you figure it out?" asked Dieter coldly. He straightened his crumpled shirt.

"The headmaster. He knew what you had used in the trick on Heff," whispered Sasha.

"R—Ralph must have told him," stuttered Dieter.

"No," said Sasha firmly. He looked up at Dieter. "Ralph never knew."

15
Toward the Goal

Sasha tiptoed down the steps before dawn the next morning. He didn't want to wake the family. Pale silver light slanted across the back stairwell. He quietly slipped into the kitchen. Sasha was surprised to see his family busy preparing breakfast together.

"Sasha run today," stated Larik from his chair. He stuffed more porridge into his face.

"I didn't want to wake anyone," said Sasha.

"You don't think we would miss the big track meet," Laddy said.

Poppy smiled as she packed a picnic in a large basket. "I'll say a prayer."

George asked, "Do you want anything to eat?"

"No," said Sasha. "I can't eat now. Save me something for after the race."

Raisa smiled. "We'll meet you there in a little while. Good luck, Sasha!"

Sasha took a deep breath. He closed the back door and headed for the track. Sasha's race was scheduled early in the meet. He was glad he didn't have to wait long.

His fingers shook as he retied his shoes for the fourth time. He walked along the track. He tried to clear his mind. He knew he was at his best. And it was a beautiful day with no wind.

Coach nodded to him. "Five minutes, Bausch."

Sasha carefully stretched each muscle. He concentrated on slowing his heartbeat. He was ready.

There were only eight racers in the event. He knew they were the best eight in Latvia. He readied himself for the start. The gun exploded, and suddenly he was running.

There were footsteps behind him and runners ahead. The first part of the lap was run in lanes. Then the racers slowly bunched. They began to spread out down the inside lane of the track.

Sasha concentrated on not pushing too soon. He wanted desperately to be in the lead. But Coach had insisted that Sasha stay in the pack for the first lap. The group seemed to move at a very quick pace. He wondered if he could hold on. Would he have anything left for the final sprint?

He settled into a comfortable pace. Now his breath came more easily. He passed two contenders. Three more still raced ahead of him. They were in the last 200-yard stretch. One contender had dropped back. The leader suddenly faded, barely able to continue running.

Keep going! Sasha willed himself to continue.

The boy next to him matched him pace for pace around the curve and into the final leg. They were gaining on the leader. Sasha knew he must pass him on the outside. He forced himself to wait until they were off the curve. He didn't want to lose precious steps.

Coach screamed at him from the sidelines, "Now, Sasha, now!" But Sasha didn't hear him.

His team stood on the sidelines, shouting, "Now, Sasha, now!" But Sasha didn't see them.

Raisa, George, and Laddy stood in the bleachers, screaming, "Now, Sasha, now!" But Sasha didn't notice them.

Poppy held the tiny cross she always wore and prayed, "Now, Sasha, now!" But Sasha didn't know.

He only saw the finish line. And he told himself not to give up. He crossed the finish line first, straining his chest against the flimsy yellow line.

Sasha sat on a bench on the sidelines. He watched the javelin throwers hurl their long sticks high into the air. Laddy sat down next to him and pounded him heartily on the back.

"I don't think I have ever been hugged so much in my life," said Sasha.

"Did you see George? He was almost crying," laughed Laddy. "We are so proud of you, Sasha."

"It feels good." Sasha smiled.

Sasha watched another javelin arch gracefully into the grass.

"Laddy, do you think it is running away to go to America? Shouldn't I stay and fight for my country? Shouldn't I stay and protect my family?" asked Sasha.

Laddy studied Sasha's serious face. He thought for a moment and then replied, "When you were running today, Sasha, were you running away or were you running toward a goal?"

16

Parade of Good-Byes

"Sasha, Sasha, can you carry me to the parade?" begged little Larik. He pulled on Sasha's coat sleeve.

"What parade?" asked Sasha. He knelt down to talk to Larik at eye level.

"The gun parade, the gun parade," squealed Larik. "Will you hold me up?"

"He's talking about the parade to commemorate the riflemen," explained Raisa, coming down the stairs. "You know, Sasha. The men who fought back the Germans during the World War. George has told you the story a hundred times."

She helped Larik into his sweater. Then she tied a flowered scarf on her head. "Do you want to come?" she asked.

"I had forgotten all about it," said Sasha. "But I promised shoulders, didn't I?"

George came down the stairs with a small red and white Latvian flag. "I thought I might wave it a bit," said George. He suddenly looked embarrassed.

"I think that's a good idea, George," agreed Sasha.

The streets were filled with people. Many of them carried small bouquets of bright flowers. Old women stood on the street corners. They offered bunches of bright blooms from their gardens for only a few **santims**.

They were soon near the parade. Sasha could hear a band playing an old Latvian song. It was a **daina**—a folk song he had learned in school. Children in traditional dress danced to the happy rhythm. Shiny black cars carried waving dignitaries. Young women waved long red and white streamers.

The honored riflemen marched next. Some of the men looked aged and gray. Two with missing limbs hobbled on crutches. Others still walked with energy, waving to the onlookers.

The crowd cheered their heroes. They showered the riflemen with flower petals.

Larik wiggled on Sasha's shoulders. "I want to be a brave soldier too," said Larik.

The parade ended at the Freedom Monument. The crowd gathered. Mounds of flowers decorated the base of the tall memorial.

President **Karlis Ulmanis** stepped from his black car. He carried a huge wreath of red and white flowers. He walked slowly toward the monument with great dignity. He lay the garland in a place of honor. The crowd clapped and cheered.

A loud bugle call silenced the crowd. Then a deep booming of drums hammered from a side street. The crowd turned expectantly.

Several hundred brown-shirted males marched toward the crowd. They marched in a strange step, keeping their legs straight at the knees. Sasha remembered the goose step from newsreels he had seen at the pictures. The drums kept an ominous beat. The crowd moved out of the marchers' path in silence.

Sasha handed Larik back to Raisa and George. He wove his way to the front of the silent crowd. He watched as row after row of stern-faced men and boys marched to the hypnotic beat. Slowly, they circled the Statue of Freedom.

In the final squadron, Dieter marched in formation, staring straight ahead. His eyes shifted to Sasha's, then away quickly. Sasha felt numb.

The commander marched at the rear of Dieter's squadron. Sasha recognized Headmaster Fleishman. His shiny-billed cap shaded fierce dark eyes. The booming drums led the formation back the way they had come. The crowd stood stunned as the drums echoed and faded.

Then Sasha turned and found his sister in the somber crowd. Raisa had handed Larik the Latvian flag. Now she pointed toward the president.

Smiling, Larik ran to the man. Larik offered the flag to the president. President Ulmanis scooped up the boy in one strong arm and lifted him toward the crowd. Larik waved the flag.

Over the noise of the fading drums, the president shouted, "Freedom! Freedom for our children!"

Sasha wandered through the narrow streets. He found himself in the square of St. Peter's Church. He needed time to think.

He began to climb to the top of the steeple. No one was around. He was breathing hard by the time he had ventured to the first lookout of the triple steeple. But there were still more flights to go.

Finally, he stood alone in the top tower. From this point, Sasha could see over the entire city. He watched as a cargo ship cast off from the dock and was tugged into midstream. A barge fought the current. The sun rested low in the sky, casting amber shafts onto the rippling water. It seemed so quiet up here—so safe.

Sasha heard movement behind him. He turned to see Dieter standing in front of him. Dieter held his military hat under his arm. His brow glistened.

"Tough climb, Dieter. You wouldn't want to mess up your fancy uniform," growled Sasha.

"Could you just listen, Sasha? I was just following orders. I didn't want to hurt anyone," explained Dieter. "When it started, I didn't know they would go after Ralph."

"Oh, were you supposed to get me?" asked Sasha.

"Not to expel you, Sasha. Not to hurt you," continued Dieter. "Just to get you to join. I told them you wouldn't be easy to recruit. They said they just wanted to pressure you a bit."

Sasha shook his head. He gazed out over the red roofs of Riga. "I will never be a part of it," he said calmly.

"I know that. I saw your face when we marched by today. So I have come to warn you. You must leave. I know your family has thought about it. Leave Latvia very soon. Go to America."

Dieter turned to go. He hesitated. Then he smiled and said, "You should have seen Fleishman's face when I told him you would never join. He smashed his favorite English teapot against the wall."

Sasha had to smile.

"Good-bye," said Sasha.

"Good-bye," replied Dieter.

The clumping of Dieter's heavy boots echoed off the narrow stairwell.

Sasha watched the sun dip below the western lowlands. It cast a fading light over forests and farms.

It is still light in America, thought Sasha. He waited until long after dark to make his way home.

Sasha put down his suitcase by the door. Poppy looked up from clearing the kitchen table.

"I came to say good-bye to you first," said Sasha.

Poppy dried her hands on her apron. "I don't want to do this again," she said.

Sasha put his arms around the plump woman and kissed her white head. "Look, I still have the St. Nicholas medal you gave me. It worked last time." Sasha tried to make his voice sound cheerful.

Poppy just nodded. "Let's go sit with your family for a moment. It will bring you luck," whispered Poppy.

Parade of Good-Byes

Master Heff stood at the end of the gangplank. Sasha shook hands with him. For the hundredth time, Sasha felt for the visa documents in his coat pocket. He needed to make sure they were still there.

Master Heff handed him a card. "Here are a few friends I know in the States. You have Ralph's address?"

"Yes," said Sasha. "Ralph says in his letter that he is not too far from my cousin's home and the school I will attend. But I looked on the map. It seems very far to me."

"America is a very big place. But I know you will be fine," insisted his teacher. "I will keep trying to get the rest of your family out."

Sasha shook George's hand. "Take care of my sister," Sasha said.

"I will," promised George.

Laddy pounded Sasha on the back. "I'll need my first mate back soon," he said. "Run for that goal."

Larik tried to pick up Sasha's suitcase. His little cheeks turned red. He wobbled a few steps. "Me come too," he said.

"Soon, Larik," said Sasha. He bent down to hug the boy. "You stay and take care of your mama and Poppy for me."

Raisa could only manage a brief smile. Sasha took his sister gently into his arms. Raisa gave him a big hug.

"I love you, Sasha."

Sasha held her and whispered, "See you soon." He hugged her twice. "One for now and one for later," he said.

Sasha turned quickly and boarded the ship. His family slowly made their way back down the dock. The great booming horn of the ocean liner blasted, echoing off the nearby square. Sasha watched from the deck as the final ropes were released. He felt movement under his feet.

A tiny tugboat muscled the ship away from the dock. Sasha studied the church steeples of Riga. Each golden rooster faced the sea, predicting fair weather as he escaped the brewing storm.

Larik tugged at his mother's hand. "Mama, where is Sasha going?"

Raisa replied, "Where he belongs."

Glossary

Alexander Victorovich Bausch people in Russia are given a first, second, and last name. The second name is their father's first name with an ending. *Ovich* means "son of" (Alexander Victorovich). *Onova* means "daughter of" (Madame Lazaronova).

babushka grandmother

borscht beet and red cabbage soup; served hot or cold

Chamberlain, Neville the British prime minister who took Britain into World War II. His belief that Hitler was a rational statesman led to the policy of appeasement toward Nazi Germany. The policy was later abandoned when Hitler invaded Czechoslovakia in 1939.

Cheka the military secret police force used by Stalin during his reign of terror

daina a Latvian folk song

gulag the prison system in Russia consisting of labor camps

gymnasium a German high school

headmaster a principal of a school

Herr a German title that means the same as "Mr."

GLOSSARY

Hitler, Adolf the leader of the Nazi Party who came to power in Germany in 1932. His totalitarian rule lasted until the end of World War II (1944). At the height of his power, he controlled most of Europe and was responsible for the deaths of millions.

kistka a tool used to apply beeswax when decorating a Russian Easter egg

kulak any Russian farmer who had other people working for him. Kulaks were killed or forced from their homes after the revolution.

kulich a traditional sweet bread baked in a tall cylinder, topped with sweet icing or sugar

paskha a sweetened, creamy cheese usually molded into a fancy shape

piroshki a fried or baked pastry with meat or vegetables inside

purges when the Russian government, led by Joseph Stalin, sought to rid itself of political enemies through imprisonment, execution, and deportation

Riga the capital city of Latvia

GLOSSARY

samovar a vessel, usually metal, used to heat water for tea. A cylinder in the middle holds burning coal. A small teapot sits on the top of the samovar to hold a strong brew.

santim a unit of Latvian currency (100 santims = 1 lat; 1 lat = approximately $1.70 in U.S. currency)

Stalin, Joseph the Communist leader who came to power after the death of Lenin. This powerful dictator ruled the Soviet Union from 1929 until 1953. He is believed to have been responsible for the deaths of millions of Russians through purges and starvation.

Ukraine an agricultural district known for its fertile soil in central Russia

Ulmanis, Karlis the president of Latvia from 1936 to 1940. He was removed from office during the Soviet invasion in 1940.

visa official permission to visit another country

DATE DUE			
OE 1 0			
DE 15 03			
AP 15 '05			
MY 3 '05			